There's a new girl in school,
but she's not like the others.

Miss Haversham had been talking for about ten minutes when it started to rain! The sky was still blue. The sun was still shining. But huge, splashy drops of water were pouring down around the school. Loud, crackly flashes of lightning were splitting open the sky. The thunder was so loud that it drowned Miss Haversham out. Then, just as suddenly as the rain had begun, it stopped. And at the same moment, the door opened and a girl walked into the classroom.

What the students of Miss Haversham's class noticed first about the girl was her flaming red hair. But what they whispered about was her clothes. In an ankle-length black dress and pointy black shoes, she looked just like a witch!

THREE LITTLE WITCHES

DEBRA HESS

HarperPaperbacks
A Division of HarperCollins*Publishers*

For Sandy, with love

HarperPaperbacks   *A Division of* HarperCollins*Publishers*
          10 East 53rd Street, New York, N.Y. 10022

Produced by Chardiet Unlimited Inc.
33 West 17th Street, New York, New York 10011.

RL 2.5 IL 008-010
First printing: August 1991

Printed in the United States of America

HarperPaperbacks and colophon are trademarks of
HarperCollins*Publishers*

10 9 8 7 6 5 4 3 2

One

Susan Cooper's eyes flew open. She sat up in bed, shaking all over. Outside, the wind howled and lightning split open the sky. Rain poured in through the open window. Susan clutched her bear tightly and looked around the room. What made her wake up? Why was she so afraid? There had been rainstorms before. Susan liked gloomy, rain-filled nights. She liked to curl up under the covers with her stuffed bear, Barney, and imagine that they were in charge of the thunder. She liked to peek out from under the covers and watch the lightning zigzag through the trees. When rainstorms started in the middle of the night, Susan almost always slept through them.

1

But there was something different about this stormy night. Something spooky.

Suddenly, Susan knew what was wrong. It was an eerie, unearthly moan. It rose above the sound of the storm and the crack of the lightning bolts. It was like nothing Susan had ever heard before. And it was coming from the courtyard beneath Susan's bedroom window.

Slowly, Susan rose from her bed and tiptoed to the window. She couldn't imagine what could be making the sound. No one had lived in the house across the courtyard for many years. The old Cranshaw mansion on Ivy Court had been empty for as long as Susan and her family had lived in Brooklyn. When the moon was full, Susan could see across the courtyard through the windows of the house. Cobwebs covered the walls and ceilings. Dead vines hung from the roof. It was the scariest place in the neighborhood. None of the kids wanted to go near the old mansion. Once, on Halloween, Susan and her best friend, Jenna, had walked past the old house and had seen dozens of black cats hanging around. Everyone thought the house was haunted. Susan knew that was ridiculous. Only babies believed in haunted houses. But now when Susan looked out the window, she gasped.

In the dead garden of the Cranshaw house stood two women dressed in black. One was tall and skinny, with a long hooked nose. The other was short and round. Both women wore long black capes that swirled in the wind. They chanted over the dead garden and cried out words that Susan had never heard before. The tall one waved her arms in circles while the short one sprinkled liquid from a jar on the ground. But the thing that amazed Susan the most was this: in the middle of a thunderstorm, with rain pouring down in buckets around them, both of the women were dry. Because, even though it was raining, it didn't rain on them!

Susan watched in fear as the women raised their arms to the sky. She thought about waking her brother, Alex. His room was right across the hall from her bedroom.

But she was afraid that if she left the window, the women might disappear. Then, suddenly, it was over. The eerie sound was gone. The rain stopped, and the moon lit up the dead garden where only moments ago the two women had stood. Susan opened her window and leaned out, looking for some sign of them. But the only thing she saw was a black cat. It was the biggest cat Susan had ever seen. It had huge, glowing green eyes. And it was looking straight at her. Susan dove into her bed, grabbed Barney, and pulled the covers over her head.

When she woke in the morning and looked out the window, everything looked just as it always had looked. Susan was sure that the storm and the mysterious women had been part of a dream.

Two

"Hi, Mom! Did you hear the thunderstorm last night?" Susan asked as she sat down to breakfast.

"What thunderstorm?" asked Mrs. Cooper, turning from the kitchen sink. Her smile quickly turned into a frown.

"Susan! Is that what you're wearing the first day of school?"

"What's wrong with what I'm wearing?" said Susan, looking down at her overalls. Susan had a closet full of clothes, but she wore her favorite overalls almost every day. They were loose and comfortable, and she could run around and climb trees in them without worrying about getting dirty.

"I just thought you might want to wear

6

one of those pretty new dresses we bought last week," said Mrs. Cooper, grabbing her car keys off the table. "I've got to run, honey. You'll have to get breakfast for yourself. I left your lunch in a bag in the fridge. Have a nice day at school." Mrs. Cooper kissed her daughter on the head and raced out of the house, almost running smack into Jenna Ross, who was coming in the door.

"Hi, Mrs. Cooper." Jenna smiled.

"Hi, Jenna," Mrs. Cooper called over her shoulder as she ran out the door.

"Wow," said Jenna. "What happened to your mom?"

"She got a job," said Susan, peering into an empty box of cereal.

"So what?" said Jenna. "She got the job two months ago. She seemed a lot calmer this summer."

"She was a lot calmer until this *morning*," said Susan, grabbing a chocolate-frosted doughnut out of a tin on the counter. Stuffing the doughnut in her mouth, she moved toward the refrigerator. She opened the door to the fridge and got her lunch out.

"I think it's just a matter of her getting used to working and getting us off to school at the same time," said Susan. She opened the brown paper bag and looked in. Then she made a face. "Egg salad. Yuck! I'm going to have to start making my own lunches, too."

Jenna laughed.

"Let me just get my jacket and we can go," said Susan, leaving the room. She reappeared a moment later, wearing a jacket and shoving her long brown hair into a baseball cap.

"Is that what you're wearing?" asked Jenna.

"What's wrong with what I'm wearing?" Susan looked hurt.

"Oh . . . uh . . . nothing," said Jenna.

"Come on, tell me. My mother said the same thing. What's wrong with what I'm wearing?"

Jenna spoke carefully. "It's just that overalls and your baseball cap were fine for

8

running around this summer. But for school . . . You know, it's the first day of the fourth grade and all . . ." Jenna's voice trailed off.

Susan looked at Jenna's carefully put-together outfit and at her own ripped overalls, then thought about it for a minute. "The way I look at it," she finally said, "is that I'm not looking forward to school, so I might as well like what I'm wearing."

Jenna smiled. "Okay, have it your way. Let's go. I'm excited."

Jenna hummed as they walked along.

"What are you in such a good mood about?" asked Susan.

"You know, Susan," said Jenna, "some of us really like school. Especially the first day."

"What's so great about the first day of school?" Susan kicked a pile of dead leaves.

"Why are you so grouchy?" asked Jenna.

"I'm not grouchy," Susan said grouchily.

"Tell the truth, Suz. Why aren't you excited about school?"

"Egg salad for lunch," said Susan.

"I love egg salad," said Jenna. "I've got peanut butter and jelly. We can trade."

"Homework," said Susan.

"Nobody gives homework on the first day of school," said Jenna.

"Annabelle Sloan," said Susan.

Now, there was a reason not to go to school! Annabelle Sloan was the most popular girl in the whole class. She was pretty and had great clothes and her mother never made her bring egg salad to school. Everyone liked Annabelle. At least, everyone pretended to like Annabelle. If Annabelle Sloan didn't like you, she made your life miserable. And the person she made the most miserable was Susan Cooper.

"She makes fun of you because you let her," said Jenna as they turned the corner.

"She makes fun of you, too," said Susan. "You just never hear her because your head is always stuck in a book."

"I hear her," said Jenna. "I just pretend I don't so she'll leave me alone. She makes fun of a lot of people. You just have to ignore her so she'll go away."

"I can't help it," said Susan. "She makes me so mad!"

Jenna put her arm around her best friend. "Cheer up, Suz. There are two fourth-grade classes this year. Maybe she won't be in ours."

The girls walked toward the entrance to Park Street Elementary School. Susan brightened up. That was the nicest thing anyone had said to her all morning. Maybe Annabelle wouldn't be in her class this year. Maybe she wouldn't be in school at all! Maybe she had switched schools, or moved out of the state, or the country, or . . .

Susan stopped in the middle of her thought. From across the crowded schoolyard, Annabelle Sloan was making a path straight for Susan. And she had an awfully mean look on her face.

Three

"She's heading straight for us," whispered Susan.

"Just ignore her," said Jenna. "Let's go sit down."

But it was too late.

"Hi, girls," Annabelle sang out loudly. She was standing right in front of them, so it was going to be hard to ignore her.

"Hi, Annabelle," said Susan, trying to be nice. "How was your summer?"

"Fabulous, just fabulous," said Annabelle. "Daddy took us to Europe for the whole summer. I suppose you stayed in Brooklyn?"

"Yep, all summer!" said Susan. Annabelle was the only girl in the class who had gone to Europe over the summer. Susan didn't care. She just wanted to get the day over with.

"Let's go inside, Susan," said Jenna.

Annabelle followed Susan and Jenna to their seats. A group of Annabelle's friends followed, too. Susan felt sick. Annabelle *was* in their class after all.

"I just wanted to tell you," Annabelle said loud enough for everyone to hear, "that I'm having a sleepover party this weekend."

Susan felt a knot growing in the pit of her stomach.

"But I can't invite you, Susan, because my mother says I can't invite any boys!"

The girls standing behind Annabelle started laughing. Susan felt the knot in her stomach grow tighter. She was trying to think of something nasty to say back to Annabelle when the school bell rang.

The students scrambled for their seats while a woman came in and wrote her name on the blackboard. Then she turned to the class.

"My name is Miss Haversham," she said in a high, squeaky voice. "And I'll be your homeroom teacher for this year." Susan looked over at Jenna. Jenna made a face. Miss Haversham sounded more like a mouse than a teacher. Were they going to have to listen to her awful voice all year? Well, at least she was only their homeroom teacher.

"I will also be teaching math class," Miss Haversham squeaked.

First egg salad, then Annabelle, and now Miss Haversham. This day was definitely getting worse.

Miss Haversham had been talking for about ten minutes when it started to rain. The sky was still blue. The sun was still shining. But huge, splashy drops of water were pouring down all around the school. Loud, crackling flashes of lightning were splitting open the sky. The thunder was so loud that it drowned out Miss Haversham's voice. Then, just as suddenly as the rain had begun, it stopped. And at the same mo-

ment, the door opened and a girl walked into the classroom.

What the students of Miss Haversham's class noticed first about the girl was her flaming red hair. But what they whispered about were her clothes. In a black dress and pointy black shoes, she looked just like a witch!

Of course, no one was rude enough to say anything. No one but Annabelle Sloan. "She looks like a witch." Annabelle laughed loud enough so everyone could hear. The new girl just stared at Annabelle. She stared while Miss Haversham introduced her to the class. She stared while she walked slowly to her seat. Every time that Annabelle whispered a mean comment about her, the girl stared. Every time Annabelle passed a note to a friend, the girl just turned and stared.

In the cafeteria at lunch, the new girl sat in a corner by herself.

"I feel sorry for her," said Jenna as she and Susan traded sandwiches.

"Well . . . she does look sort of like a

witch," said Susan. "And what about her name? Libby Lawson sort of sounds like a witch's name."

"So what?" answered Jenna. "You don't like it when Annabelle makes fun of you."

Susan munched on her peanut-butter-and-jelly sandwich thoughtfully. "If I were a witch," she said to Jenna, "I'd zap Annabelle into a toad."

Jenna giggled. "I'd zap her into a worm."

"Or a really disgusting, hairy rat." Susan laughed.

"Or one of those beasts with only one eye."

"Yeah, with snakes for hair."

"Uh, oh . . ." said Jenna. Susan looked up from her sandwich. Annabelle Sloan had just walked into the cafeteria, and it looked as though she was heading straight for Susan and Jenna.

But Annabelle walked right past them. With her usual circle of friends trailing behind her, Annabelle headed straight for Libby. Everyone in the cafeteria was watching.

"Hi, Lizzie," Annabelle said icily.

Libby looked up from her lunch slowly.

"Libby," she said.

"Excuse me?" Annabelle said with a nasty little smile.

"Libby," said Libby calmly. "My name is Libby."

The girls behind Annabelle giggled.

"What kind of a name is Libby?" said Annabelle.

"It's my name," said Libby. "Do you have a problem with it?"

"Oh, no," Annabelle said in her snobbiest voice. "It's just . . . where exactly do you come from?"

Libby's face broke into a funny little grin. "I come from a galaxy far, far away," she said.

Annabelle's friends laughed. But this time, they weren't laughing at Libby. They were laughing at her joke. Annabelle didn't think it was funny. The only jokes she wanted anyone to laugh at were the ones she made. Annabelle leaned over the table and brought her face close to Libby's.

"Listen, *Lily*," she snarled. "Just remember that I make the jokes around here. And the only thing I see to laugh at is the stupid dress you have on. Don't you think it's a little early for Halloween?"

Libby looked as if she'd been punched in the stomach. And that was exactly what Annabelle wanted. Satisfied, Annabelle walked away. Her group of friends followed, giggling and whispering as they sat down at an empty table.

Libby just stared at Annabelle. She stared for a really long time. She was still staring when Annabelle opened her designer lunchbox and a mouse ran out.

Annabelle screamed. Annabelle's friends screamed. Susan and Jenna laughed. Libby sat alone silently, with an odd little grin on her face.

Four

"Wow!" said Alex. "How did she get the mouse in there?"

Alex was Susan's younger brother. He was in the third grade and a computer whiz. Susan's mother said Alex had a bottomless pit for a stomach and the table manners of a pig.

"I didn't say she put the mouse in Annabelle's lunch," said Susan. "I just said a mouse ran out of the lunchbox."

"It sounds to me like she put the mouse in there," Alex said as he shoveled meat loaf into his mouth.

"Don't eat so fast, Alex," said Susan's mother. Mrs. Cooper was always telling Alex not to eat so fast.

"I'm a growing boy, Mom," said Alex, stuffing potatoes into his mouth.

"Yeah, but in what direction are you growing?" Susan and her father said at almost exactly the same time. Everyone laughed. It was the same conversation they had every night at dinner.

"I hear that someone has moved into the old Cranshaw place," said Mr. Cooper. Susan almost choked on her food, thinking about the dream she had had the night before.

"You're kidding," said Alex. "Who would want to live in that creepy place?"

"I don't know," answered Mr. Cooper, "but someone does. The house was sold last week."

"Witches used to live in that house," said Alex, helping himself to another piece of meat loaf.

"Don't be silly," said Susan's mother. "There's no such thing as a witch."

"Oh, yeah?" said Alex. "What about that creepy new kid in Susan's class?"

"I didn't say she was a witch, Alex," Su-

21

san snapped. "I said she dressed like a witch. There's a difference."

"What's the difference?" asked Alex.

"The difference is that there's no such thing as a witch. Like Mom said," Susan told her brother. But all she could think about were the two strange women in black from her dream.

"Well, I'm going to bake a cake or something to take over there and welcome them to the neighborhood," said Mrs. Cooper.

"Why?" asked Alex.

"To be neighborly, of course," Mrs. Cooper said. "Alex, stop shoveling your food!"

The next day after school, Jenna and Susan went to Susan's house to play. There was a cake in the kitchen with a note attached to it.

Susan—I went to pick Alex up at a friend's. I came home early today and baked a cake. Please bring it over to the new neighbors. Introduce yourself and say welcome to the neighborhood.

See you at dinner.

—Mom

"I'm not going over there with you," said Jenna.

"You have to," said Susan. "You can't make me go alone. Besides, it will be an adventure."

"Well, okay," Jenna agreed. "But I'm not going inside."

The girls carried the cake over to the old Cranshaw place. The house looked the same as it had always looked. There were dead vines and cobwebs on the outside, and the house was dark. Slowly, the girls climbed the front steps to the door.

"There's no one here," said Jenna. "Let's go!"

"We have to ring the bell and make sure," said Susan nervously.

"Why?" said Jenna. "There's no one here."

An eerie moan came from inside the house. Jenna jumped.

"Still think there's no one in there?" asked Susan.

"Nothing human," whispered Jenna.

Susan didn't want her best friend to

23

know that she was scared, too. So she took a deep breath and rang the bell.

"See—there's no one here. Let's go," said Jenna.

Footsteps sounded in the house. Jenna started running down the stairs.

"Wait a minute," said Susan, grabbing her friend.

The footsteps stopped. Susan and Jenna held their breath. The door opened with a creak, and a large black cat ran out. Jenna gave a little cry. She would have run that instant, but Susan held her back. Standing in the darkened doorway, in the middle of the cobwebs and dead vines, was Libby Lawson.

Five

"Hi," said Libby, smiling at the two girls. "Aren't you two in my class at school?"

"Uh . . . hi," Susan said, trying not to stare into the house. "I . . . uh . . . here!" Susan shoved the cake at Libby. "It's from my mother. She says 'welcome to the neighborhood.' "

"Thank you," Libby said politely, taking the cake.

The three girls stood in silence, looking each other over. Finally, Libby spoke.

"I'm Libby."

Susan smiled. "I'm Susan. And this is Jenna."

"Hi," said Jenna shyly.

"Do you *live* here?" asked Susan rudely. Jenna kicked her in the leg.

"I mean," continued Susan, "do you live here alone?"

Libby smiled sweetly. "No. I live here with my Aunt Harriet and my Aunt Aurora," she said. "Would you like to come in and meet them?"

"We have to go now. Maybe another time," Jenna practically yelled.

"Don't be ridiculous, Jenna," said Susan, grabbing Jenna's arm. Then she turned to Libby. "We would love to see your house and meet your aunts."

Libby held open the door, and the two girls entered the house. Susan didn't know what she had expected to see, but she had to admit that it looked like a normal house. The cobwebs had been brushed away, and there was furniture in the once-empty rooms. Libby led them down a hallway to the kitchen. "Won't you sit down?" she said. Then she excused herself and went to get her aunts.

"It seems like an okay house," Susan whispered after Libby had left the room.

"I know," Jenna whispered back. "But don't you think Libby is a little strange?"

Susan nodded her head. "Yes. But she seems nice, too."

"Susan, look!" Jenna pointed to a huge black cat that had wandered into the room. "Have you ever seen a cat that big?"

Susan took one look at the cat and almost jumped out of her seat. It was the cat from her dream. It had to be. It had the same black silky fur and glowing green eyes. Susan was about to tell Jenna about her dream when Libby walked into the room with one of her aunts.

"Susan and Jenna," said Libby, "this is my Aunt Harriet."

"How do you do, my dear," said Aunt Harriet, putting out her hand for Susan to shake. But Susan didn't shake her hand. She didn't move a muscle. She just stared at Libby's Aunt Harriet. She had seen her before. Aunt Harriet was the short, round witch she had seen the other night!

Six

"Is something wrong, dear?" Aunt Harriet asked.

"Uh, no. Not at all," said Susan, forcing herself to smile.

"Well, then," said Aunt Harriet. "How about a little snack? Would you like some of that cake your mother sent over?"

Susan looked over at the cat. Now it was curled up on the table, and it was staring straight at her with twinkling eyes. Susan wasn't sure, but she thought the cat winked at her. She sprang up from her chair.

"We can't stay for cake. I promised my mother I'd come right home," Susan said. Jenna looked surprised.

"Well, all right. Maybe another time,"

Aunt Harriet said kindly. "Libby, why don't you see your friends to the door?"

The minute Libby closed the front door, Susan grabbed Jenna's hand and the two girls raced back to the Coopers' house. They ran up the steps of the brownstone and didn't stop until they were in Susan's bedroom with the door closed. Susan went straight to the window and pulled down the shade.

"Susan—what's wrong?" asked Jenna. "Why did we have to run home?"

"There's something weird going on over there," Susan told her friend.

Susan told Jenna about her dream of the witches in the garden. Jenna listened very carefully until Susan was done. Then she went to the window. She lifted the shade and peeked out. When she was done looking, she turned to Susan.

"I don't see any witches out there now." Jenna grinned.

"They aren't going to come out during the daytime," Susan explained.

"How do you know?" asked Jenna.

"It's just one of those things everyone knows about witches," Susan told her friend.

"What are the other things?" Jenna asked.

"Oh, you know. They ride on broomsticks and do mean things to people and stuff like that."

"I don't know, Suz. I mean, I know the house is really scary and everything. But do you really think Libby is a witch?"

"All I know is that I saw Aunt Harriet in the garden last night," said Susan.

"That doesn't prove anything."

"What about the other aunt?"

"What about her?"

"She was the cat on the kitchen table."

"Now who's being weird?" said Jenna.

"She was in the garden, Jen. The exact same cat was in the garden last night."

"How do you know it was the same cat?" asked Jenna.

"For one thing, it's the biggest cat I've ever seen. For another thing, it has those huge glowing eyes."

31

"You know," said Jenna, "that same cat was in the schoolyard today."

Susan nodded her head. "And Libby was talking to it!"

"Well, we'd better stay away from that house from now on," said Jenna.

"No way!" said Susan.

"What if they really are witches?" asked Jenna. "We don't want them to find out that we know."

"They already know," said Susan. "The cat winked at me!"

"I think we should just forget about it," said Jenna.

Susan knew her friend was scared. But there was no way she was going to forget about it. If there were witches living in the Cranshaw mansion on Ivy Court, Susan Cooper was going to find out.

Seven

When Susan woke the next morning and looked out her window, she could hardly believe her eyes. The Cranshaw mansion was gone! It hadn't disappeared, but Susan could no longer see the house from her room. A row of the biggest daisies that Susan had ever seen had sprung from the dead garden overnight!

Susan opened her window and leaned out. The daisy petals moved softly in the early-morning breeze. Susan gasped. Each petal was the size of a dinner plate, and the flowers reached up into the sky, almost to the top of the building. Between the flowers, Susan could see rows of bushes. There were raspberry bushes and blackberry bushes, and bushes with berries Susan had never seen before. From cracks in what looked like newly laid cement, little blue flowers sprang from the ground. The air smelled like fresh herbs. Susan dressed as quickly as she could and ran downstairs to find her mother. But Mrs. Cooper only had time to kiss her daughter goodbye before she left for work.

Susan ate breakfast as quickly as she could. She wanted to get to school so she could tell Jenna about the garden. She ran most of the way, but Jenna hadn't gotten to school yet. So Susan took her seat.

"Oh, Suuuusan!" Susan heard the whine before she saw anyone coming toward her. She tried to ignore Annabelle, but it didn't work. The louder Annabelle whined her name, the madder Susan got, until finally Susan shouted, "WHAT?" Which was exactly what Annabelle wanted her to do, of course.

"I was just wondering if you cut off all your hair this summer," Annabelle said in a sickly sweet voice. "You've had that stupid cap on this whole week, and I thought maybe it was because you cut your hair. Or maybe you were sick and it all fell out." Annabelle started giggling and turned to her friends. "Can you imagine what Susan would look like bald?" she drawled. Then, in one swift motion, Annabelle ripped the cap off and Susan's long brown hair fell around her shoulders.

"Give it back," Susan said, reaching for the cap.

"Make me," said Annabelle, holding the cap up high. Susan didn't know what to do. She was pretty sure she could beat Annabelle up if it came down to it. But then she'd get into trouble, and her mother would be called into the principal's office, and Annabelle would have one more reason to say Susan was acting like a boy. It just didn't seem worth it.

Annabelle was looking into the cap. "It must be dirty in here," she said, "since you never take it off your head. Do you ever wash your hair?" But before Susan could think of anything mean to say, Annabelle

screamed. A giant hairy bug had crawled out of the cap and up Annabelle's arm.

The class was in an uproar! Annabelle hopped around the room, screaming for someone to get the bug off of her. Herbie Beanfield, who loved bugs, came to the rescue. He scooped the furry spider off Annabelle and brought it to his desk to look at it more closely. One by one, the kids in the class quieted down and took their seats.

Susan was upset. But more than anything, she was curious. Just before the bug had crawled out of the cap, Susan had looked over at the door to the classroom. Libby Lawson was standing there. She was staring at Annabelle with a funny little grin on her face. It was the same little grin Susan had seen when the mouse had crawled out of Annabelle's lunchbox.

Eight

"I just know Libby made that spider crawl out of my cap," Susan told Jenna as they walked home from school.

"Of all the days to be late to homeroom," Jenna said. "I wish I could have seen Annabelle's face!"

Susan smiled. "That's twice in one week that I got to see Annabelle scream. I don't care if Libby is a witch. Anyone who can make Annabelle do that is okay with me."

Jenna giggled. "Me, too, I guess."

Jenna started to turn onto the street where Susan lived, but Susan stopped her.

"Let's go to Libby's house," she said.

"What?" cried Jenna. "Are you crazy?"

"I want to show you something," Susan told her best friend.

"I'm not going over there," said Jenna.

"You just said you didn't mind if Libby was a witch," Susan reminded her.

"I said I didn't mind if she does mean things to Annabelle Sloan. That doesn't mean I want to go over to her house," said Jenna. "Besides, I've been thinking about it. Maybe what you saw that night in the garden really was a dream."

"Then why don't you want to go over to the house?" asked Susan, smiling.

"Okay, okay," said Jenna. "I'll go. But only if you tell me why."

"The garden," said Susan as she dragged Jenna in the direction of Libby's house.

"You mean that same dead garden where you dreamed there were witches?"

"I mean the same garden where I *saw* the witches," said Susan. "Except that it isn't dead anymore. There are hundreds of flowers in it now!"

"That's impossible," said Jenna. "There

wasn't a flower in it last night. I looked out your window. I'm sure of it!"

"Exactly!" said Susan. Then she pulled Jenna all the way to Libby's house.

Susan and Jenna were trying to figure out the best way to sneak around the house when Aunt Harriet opened the door.

"Hello, girls. Would you like to see Libby?" Aunt Harriet asked kindly. "She's out in the garden, I believe."

It was the most amazing garden the girls had ever seen. Giant roses and daffodils arched up into the sky. The petals of the giant daisies formed a curtain around the garden. The air was filled with the scent of flowers and herbs.

"It doesn't look very witchy to me," whispered Jenna. "I think they just hired a great gardener."

"Just wait," said Susan. "What do you want to bet we find Libby chanting some weird spell or something?" Susan stopped in her tracks. Libby was sitting on a bench in the middle of the garden. She had her head in her hands, and she was crying.

Nine

"Maybe we should go," whispered Jenna.

"Yeah, maybe you're right," said Susan.

Just then, Libby looked up. She quickly dried her eyes and rose to greet her new classmates.

"Sorry if we're bothering you," began Susan. "Your aunt let us in. I guess we came at a bad time."

Susan turned to leave. Jenna was right behind her.

"Please stay," said Libby. "Would you like some lemonade?"

While Libby went inside the house to get lemonade, Susan and Jenna looked around the garden.

"Wow," said Jenna. "I see what you mean."

"If they aren't witches, how did they do it?" whispered Susan.

Jenna shrugged her shoulders and looked around. There *was* something peculiar about the way the garden had sprung up overnight. Not only that, but some of the flower stalks were so tall that neither of the girls could reach the petals. Susan was trying to climb up one of the stalks when Libby reappeared.

"My aunts are quite good gardeners," said Libby, putting the tray with the lemonade and glasses on a small table that Susan was sure hadn't been there before.

Susan slid down the flower stalk and fell to the ground. A giant flower petal came loose and fell softly through the air, landing on her. Jenna ran to pull the petal off of her friend. The two girls looked at each other with wide eyes. There was definitely something weird going on.

Libby poured the lemonade and handed a glass to each of her new friends. Then the three girls sat in the shade of a wild, up-side-down buttercup.

Susan looked down at the lemonade in her glass. It was the thickest lemonade she had ever seen.

"What kind of lemonade is this?" Susan asked Libby.

"I made it myself!" said Libby. "I use whole lemons so it tastes better. My aunt taught me how to make it!" Libby brought her glass to her lips and took a mouthful of the lemonade. Then she seemed to chew it. She swallowed, and smiled at her friends.

"Try it," said Libby. "It's really much better this way."

Susan looked at Jenna. She was picking pits out of her lemonade. Then Susan glanced down at the glass in her own hand. The liquid in her glass didn't look at all like the lemonade she was used to drinking. In fact, it didn't look like liquid at all. It looked like a mess of lemon rind and pits and pulp. There was hardly any lemon juice at all. Susan decided to change the subject.

"I know it's none of my business," said Susan, "but how come you were crying when we came in?"

"SUSAN!" Jenna said loudly.

"I'm sorry," Susan said. "I was just trying to see if we could help, that's all." Susan looked into her lemonade. She was really getting thirsty. Maybe if she pulled out some of the rind, it would look better. She reached into the glass, but noticed that Libby was watching her. Susan dropped the rind back in her glass.

"Can we help?" Susan asked, a little more gently this time.

Libby shrugged her shoulders. "I don't know. It's nothing, really. It's just . . . I guess I just have a little trouble making new friends," she said sadly. Then she took another mouthful of lemonade and chewed it.

"Everyone has trouble making friends sometimes," Jenna told her gently.

"Not sometimes," said Libby. "I *always* have trouble making friends. And the other kids pick on me. Like that mean Annabelle. What's wrong with her, anyway?"

Susan and Jenna laughed. "She picks on everyone," said Susan. "You and I are just two of her favorites."

"I noticed that today," Libby said thoughtfully. "It was very mean of her to pull your hat off. Someone really ought to teach that girl a lesson. . . ." Susan noticed that Libby was getting that funny look on her face again. Her green eyes were twinkling. The corner of the right side of her mouth was smiling. Susan wondered how she did that.

The three girls sat silently in the garden, dreaming of ways to get back at Annabelle Sloan. After a few minutes, Libby left the garden to get some cookies. The second she was out of sight, Susan and Jenna started whispering.

"She's chewing her lemonade," said Susan.

"Of course she's chewing it," said Jenna. "How else is she going to drink it?"

Susan grinned at her friend. "I guess this is the way witches drink their lemonade."

"Very funny," said Jenna.

"I'm not kidding," said Susan, looking into her glass. "Why else would she drink this stuff?"

"I don't know," said Jenna. "Maybe she really likes it."

The two girls stared at Libby's lemonade.

"Maybe we should try it," said Susan. "I'm really thirsty."

"Me, too," said Jenna. "But let's do it before she gets back, so we can spit it out if we need to."

Susan took a deep breath and brought the glass to her lips. Then she took a mouthful of the lemonade just the way she had seen Libby do it. She chewed for a while and then swallowed.

"Well?" asked Jenna. "How is it?"

"Not bad," said Susan, taking another mouthful. "Not bad at all."

"You're kidding," said Jenna. Then she tasted her own lemonade. She chewed for a moment, spit out a pit, and then swallowed.

"Hey," said Jenna. "There's sugar in this. Lots of sugar."

"Yeah," said Susan. "And something else I don't think I've ever tasted before."

"It's good!" said Jenna, taking another mouthful.

"Really good!" said Susan, still chewing. "But I still think she's a witch."

"She is not."

"Is too."

"Prove it!"

"Okay, I will!" said Susan.

"How?" asked Jenna.

"I'm not sure," said Susan, chewing her lemonade. "If we could just spend some time with her, maybe she would slip up and do something. . . ."

"Hey, that's not a bad idea," said Jenna. "Maybe we can—"

"Shhh." Susan stopped her friend from saying anything else. "She's coming back."

"So," said Libby, putting a plate of cookies on the table, "what are we going to do about Annabelle?"

"Well, I have an idea," said Jenna, pouring herself another glass of Libby's lemonade.

"What kind of idea?" asked Libby.

"I think I know of a way to make Annabelle stop making fun of both of you. We have to give her less to pick on."

"How?" Susan and Libby spoke at the same time.

"What does Annabelle make fun of the most?" Jenna asked.

"That's easy," said Susan. "My clothes."

"I guess it's the same with me," said Libby.

"Well, I hope you don't mind my saying it," said Jenna, "but Susan . . . you dress too sloppily. And Libby . . . well, you don't dress the same way as most people around here. I think we should go shopping!"

"Shopping?" said Susan. "Yuck!"

"Why not?" said Jenna, shooting a dirty

look at Susan. "It'll be fun. We can get you both great-looking new clothes. Then Annabelle won't be able to make fun of the way either of you dresses. We can walk over to Hamilton Square, where all the stores are. And after we're done clothes shopping, we can have lunch. It'll be great."

"Okay," Susan said. "Maybe it will be fun. I'll have to ask my mother."

"I don't know if my aunts will let me," said Libby.

"Forget it," said Jenna. "It was just an idea."

"But I'll ask," said Libby. She was starting to look excited. "It really might be fun!"

Jenna and Susan looked at each other. This was perfect! A whole day shopping on Saturday with Libby would prove once and for all whether or not she was a witch.

Ten

On Saturday morning, the sun shone brightly. The three girls headed for Hamilton Square. Susan bought a pair of light-blue corduroy overalls with little flowers all over it. Libby bought a couple of skirts and tops that Jenna picked out for her. None of the clothes that Libby bought were black.

When they were done shopping, Susan suggested that they go to the deli for lunch.

"I thought we'd have a picnic, instead," said Libby.

"That's a great idea," Susan agreed. "But we forgot to bring picnic stuff."

There was that strange little smile again. "I brought everything we need," said Libby, pointing at the knapsack on her back. Susan looked over at Jenna. What witchy things was Libby carrying in her knapsack?

The girls walked to a small park nearby. Libby pulled an enormous blanket from the knapsack and spread it out for them to sit on.

"I wondered what was in there," Jenna said.

"How did you fit this blanket in your knapsack?" asked Susan, stretching out on the blanket.

"You'd be surprised if you knew how much room there was in this thing," said Libby.

Susan was pretty sure that nothing having to do with Libby was going to surprise her. She looked over at Jenna as if to say "now you're going to see some real witch-craft." Jenna rolled her eyes.

"So," said Libby, sitting down. "What do you want for lunch?"

"What have you got?" asked Jenna.

"What do you want?" repeated Libby.

"How about peanut butter sandwiches,

potato chips, and chocolate milk," said Susan.

"You would eat that every day if you could." Jenna laughed.

"Wouldn't you?" asked Susan.

"Sure. Why not." Jenna was always agreeable.

"Okay," said Libby, staring into her knapsack. "Three peanut butter sandwiches coming up!" Libby stared into her knapsack for another few seconds. Then she reached in and pulled out three sandwiches, three bags of potato chips, and a jug of lemonade.

"I don't have any chocolate milk," she said as she handed the sandwiches and chips to Susan and Jenna. "I hope you like lemonade."

Now it was Jenna's turn to shoot Susan a meaningful look. After all, what kind of a witch wouldn't be able to turn lemonade into chocolate milk? Susan would have to come up with a lot more proof before Jenna would believe that Libby was a witch.

"I can't believe you knew what we

would want to eat," Susan said as she unwrapped her sandwich.

Libby smiled. "Like you said, Susan, who wouldn't want to eat peanut butter sandwiches every day?"

Susan smiled and finished unwrapping her sandwich. It seemed a little lumpy to her, but she didn't want to hurt Libby's feelings. Susan bit into her sandwich. At first she couldn't say exactly what was wrong. Then she looked over at Jenna, who was chewing slowly, a puzzled look on her face. It took a few moments, but Susan finally figured out what was wrong with the sandwich. It was peanut butter, all right. It was a butter sandwich with peanuts stuck in it!

"I know what you're going to say," Jenna said later that day. They had just dropped Libby off and were walking toward Susan's house. "The sandwich was disgusting. But that just makes her a little weird. It still doesn't prove that she's a witch."

Eleven

On Monday, Libby didn't show up at school. Annabelle tried to make fun of Susan's new overalls, but the other kids in class liked them so much that Susan didn't let Annabelle bother her. After school, Susan and Jenna decided to go over to Libby's house to see what was wrong.

"I hope she isn't sick," said Jenna as they walked up the steps of Libby's house.

"Maybe her aunts were mad about her new clothes and wouldn't let her wear them," said Susan.

"Maybe she heard you call her a witch and didn't want to see you again," teased Jenna.

"She *is* a witch," said Susan.

Susan rang the bell, but no one came to the door. After a few minutes, Susan knocked. When no one answered, she tried the doorknob. The door swung open and Susan started to walk into the house.

"Susan, maybe no one is home," said Jenna. "I don't think we should just walk in without being invited."

"Come on. It'll be an adventure," said Susan.

Jenna groaned. "Not another adventure." But she followed Susan into the house anyway.

"Hello," Susan called as they entered. No one answered. The two girls walked farther into the house.

"Let's go check out the garden," said Susan, walking through the kitchen.

But as they went through the kitchen on the way to the garden, they heard a sound. It was like a dull moan, and it was coming from the basement.

"What's that sound?" whispered Jenna, her voice shaking.

"I don't know," said Susan. "But it

doesn't sound human." The girls moved closer to the sound. As they reached the basement door, the moan became a chant. Susan pressed her ear against the basement door. The chanting was clearer, but she couldn't make out the words. Very, very slowly, Susan opened the basement door. The two girls peered into the basement. What they saw made them gasp. Standing on either side of a huge cauldron, and dressed all in black, stood Libby's aunts. Roly-poly Aunt Harriet stirred a bubbling mixture with a large wooden spoon. A tall, thin woman, who the girls guessed was Aunt Aurora, chanted:

"Bubble brew of honey bee,
Bubble bark of young yew tree.
Add the spittle of a bird,
Add to that the sacred word.

"Make a cloud so small and slight,
Rain on our garden, then take flight.
Arise today from misty night,
Block out the sun and all its light.

"From near and far now hear our call,
From this cloud make raindrops fall."

Then Aunt Aurora raised her arms to the sky and cried out: *"Mamborundamo!"*

Susan and Jenna heard a crack of thunder. A moment later, a cloud formed over the cauldron and drifted out the basement window into the garden.

Susan wanted to race out to the garden to see if the cloud rained, but Jenna was too frightened and wanted to go home. The girls knelt by the basement door, whispering about what to do, when all of a sudden a voice called out behind them.

"Susan! Jenna! What are you doing here?" It was Libby, standing right behind them. She was wearing her black dress, and her green eyes glowed with anger.

Twelve

Susan and Jenna waited nervously in Libby's bedroom. It looked pretty much like any normal nine-year-old girl's bedroom. Except instead of stuffed bears and dolls, Libby had stuffed cats and stuffed bats and a giant stuffed spider. And sitting on her desk next to her math book was a book called *Spells*, and next to that, one called *Potions*. Susan and Jenna decided not to touch anything. Even Susan was scared now.

After Libby had found them crouched next to the basement door, she had politely asked them to wait in her bedroom while she talked to her aunts. That was half an hour ago. What was taking so long?

Finally, Libby showed up carrying a tray

with lemonade and cookies on it. Susan and Jenna each took a glass of lemonade. But neither of them wanted to touch the cookies, which were shaped like spiders.

"Go ahead. They're just regular cookies," said Libby. "This is my Aunt Aurora's idea of a joke."

"Then she isn't mad at us?" asked Susan, trying not to let her voice give away how frightened she was.

"She was furious at first," said Libby. "But when I explained to her that you were my friends and wouldn't tell anyone, she calmed down." Libby looked Susan straight in the eyes. "You won't tell anyone, will you?" she demanded.

"Tell what?" Susan practically shouted. "I didn't see anything. Did you see anything, Jenna?"

"Who, me? No. See what?" said Jenna, catching on.

Libby stared at her new friends. She looked as if she was trying to make a decision. Finally, she spoke.

"I wasn't in school today because I have

a slight cold and my aunts thought I should stay home," she said.

"Oh, is that all?" said Susan. Then she stood up. "Well, I guess we have to be going now. Thanks for the lemonade."

"Sit down, Susan," Libby said firmly. Susan sat down. Libby took a deep breath, then she continued. "We aren't sure how much you saw, but my aunts have said that it's all right for me to let you in on a little secret. It's a secret you've probably already guessed. But I need you both to promise on your word of honor that you'll never tell anyone what I'm about to tell you. Do you promise?"

"I promise," said Susan.

"I promise," whispered Jenna.

"All right, then," said Libby. Then she leaned in toward her friends and spoke very softly. "My aunts and I are part of a minority group. We are what you call . . . witches!"

"I knew it," Susan said before she could stop herself. Jenna glared at her. Libby smiled her funny little smile.

"It would be terribly dangerous for us if anyone found out," Libby said, looking hard at Susan. "People don't understand witches." Susan thought she saw tears in Libby's eyes. "We would have to move. And I'm really starting to like it here."

"We don't want you to move," said Susan. "We won't tell anyone. Promise!"

"I believe you, Susan," said Libby. "But I should also warn you that my Aunt Aurora is an incredibly powerful witch. If you slip and tell anyone, she'll know and . . ." Libby's voice trailed off. Susan shivered.

"Now," said Libby. "Do you have any questions?"

"I have a question," said Susan. "How do we know you're a witch?"

"SUSAN!" cried Jenna.

"I mean," continued Susan, "we saw your aunts do something pretty witchy, and I'm willing to believe that they're witches. But we haven't seen you do anything to prove *you're* a witch. And you have to admit you don't exactly look like a witch."

"I don't know what you mean," said Libby. "What do you want me to do?"

Susan thought for a minute. "Make something fly," she said.

Libby looked sad. "I'm not very good at flying," she said.

"Well," said Susan, "then make something disappear."

"I'm not very good at that either," answered Libby. "I'm only a beginning witch. I'm not very good at most things."

"What can you do?" asked Susan.

Libby's face broke into a smile. "I can make my stuffed animals come to life!"

"DO IT!" cried Susan and Jenna at the same time.

Libby jumped up and got one of her stuffed animals down from a shelf. It was a small bat, pitch-black in color, with small red eyes and weblike wings.

Libby sat down in the center of her bed and held the stuffed bat in both hands. She closed her eyes and concentrated. Susan and Jenna sat perfectly still, not daring to make a sound. When Libby opened her eyes, she was staring at the bat. She stared hard and she stared long. She stared for such a long time that Susan thought she had gone into a trance. And then, suddenly, with a horrible little squeak, the bat flew from Libby's hands and dove straight for Susan. Susan screamed. She covered her head and started to crawl under the bed. The bat flew up to the ceiling and dove at the floor again. By this time, Jenna was screaming, too. With a satisfied smile, Libby closed her eyes and concentrated once more. A second later, she was holding a stuffed bat in her hands again.

"Okay, okay, I believe you," said Jenna.

"That was incredible," added Susan, her eyes wide with amazement. "Can you do it with other animals?"

Libby nodded her head.

"Libby . . . did you put the mouse in Annabelle's lunch?" Jenna asked.

"I was trying for a frog," said Libby.

"And the spider?" asked Jenna.

Libby sighed. "I wasn't trying to conjure anything that time," Libby admitted. "I

was just so mad at that mean Annabelle. I was staring at her and thinking that I'd like to do something to scare her. The next thing I knew, the spider was there. I wasn't even sure I had done it."

Jenna laughed. "It was great all the same," she said. "Can you turn Annabelle into something green and slimy?"

"I don't think so," said Libby. She looked sadder than ever.

"What's the matter?" asked Jenna.

Libby shrugged. "I don't know. I guess I sort of like it here. I don't want to move."

"Why would you have to move?" asked Susan.

"I'm still not very good at being a witch," Libby said. "And every year my aunts give me a test. Last year, it was animal spells. I did okay with that, even though I still mess up a lot. This year, I flunked their test twice. If I flunk it again, they're going to send me away to a school for witches."

"Wow!" said Susan. "That would be fun!"

"Not really," Libby told her new friends.

"A girl I knew was sent to that school. She got into a fight with one of the other kids and was turned into a lizard. They never figured out how to turn her back again."

The three girls sat in silence, thinking about how life would be as a lizard. Suddenly, Susan jumped up. "I've got it!" she said. "We'll help you, Libby. Three minds are better than one. Right, Jenna?"

"I don't know . . ." said Jenna.

"Of course they are," Susan continued. "Okay, Libby, what's the test this year?"

"I don't know if I should tell you," said Libby.

"Do you want to spend your life as a lizard?" asked Susan. That was all it took.

"Okay," said Libby. "I guess it's worth a try."

"Well . . . what's the test?"

"Flying," said Libby. "I have to learn how to fly."

Thirteen

The following day after school, the three girls were sitting in the kitchen of Libby's house, munching spider cookies and chewing lemonade. All three of the friends were in a terrific mood. Libby had worn one of her new outfits to school, and all Susan and Jenna could think about was the secret they now shared with Libby. Not even Annabelle Sloan could ruin their day.

"Okay," said Susan. "How do most witches fly?"

"Brooms, of course," said Jenna. "In the movies they always fly on broomsticks."

"That's ridiculous." Libby laughed. "Broomsticks are really hard to balance on, and they get all warped when it rains."

"Well, how do witches fly?" asked Jenna.

Libby thought for a minute. "Lots of different ways," she said. "My Aunt Harriet flies by using her magic shawl."

"Great!" exclaimed Susan. "All we have to do is get you a magic shawl."

"I don't think so," said Libby. "That shawl was given to her long ago by a magician she once dated. There are no more like it in the world."

"A magician?" said Susan, her eyes wide. Libby shrugged.

"How does your other aunt fly?" asked Jenna.

"Aunt Aurora is so powerful that she doesn't need anything to fly," Libby explained. "She just thinks about it, and then she flies."

"Wow!" said Susan. "Maybe she'd teach us all how to do that!" Libby and Jenna just stared at her.

"It was just an idea," said Susan. The girls sat silently, each thinking of ways for Libby to fly.

"I'll tell you all the ways I've tried," said

Libby. "First, I tried to fly with a cape. Sort of like a bird. It worked pretty well for takeoff, but I guess I said the wrong spell over the cape, because I kept falling. That was the first test I failed. Then I tried a magic carpet, but I couldn't keep my balance."

"Wait a minute!" Jenna exclaimed. "Did you have to say a spell over the carpet, too?"

"Sure," said Libby. "You always have to say a spell over the cape or carpet you're using to fly. That gives it the power of flight if you've said the spell right."

"Can you say a spell over anything?" asked Jenna.

"Sure," said Libby. "I guess so."

"I don't suppose witches have any use for vacuum cleaners, do they?" Jenna asked Libby.

"Of course," said Libby. "We have one in the hall closet."

The three girls looked at each other, smiles breaking across their faces.

"Let's go!" said Susan. They leaped up

71

from the kitchen table. Libby led the way to a hall closet. Standing in between a broom and a mop was a shiny new upright vacuum cleaner.

A little while later, the girls stood around the vacuum cleaner. Libby chanted the spell for flight over the machine. Then she hopped on and cried out for the vacuum cleaner to fly. But nothing happened. Libby was still sitting on the vacuum cleaner on the floor of the room. She got off and looked at her friends.

"I guess this isn't going to work either," she said sadly.

"Maybe we have to plug it in," said Jenna.

Libby shrugged her shoulders and climbed back on the vacuum cleaner. She sat up front and grabbed hold of the handle.

"There's lots of room up here," she said. "Why don't one of you get on behind me."

"I will!" cried Susan, throwing her leg over the back of the machine and holding on to Libby.

Jenna bent down and plugged in the vacuum cleaner. Then she reached up and hit the "on" switch. The vacuum cleaner whirred, and a gust of air blew out the tube in the back, but nothing happened. Susan and Libby just sat on the vacuum cleaner while it sucked up the dirt in the room.

Susan was about to get off the vacuum cleaner when Libby stopped her.

"I think I need to tell it to fly again," she said. Then Libby looked down at the handle. "FLY, VACUUM CLEANER!" she called. Suddenly, the machine gave a jerk. A great gust of wind blew out of the hose, and Susan and Libby rose into the air.

"Aim the handle at the window," Jenna yelled above the roar of the wind. Libby moved the handle so that it faced the window, and the girls sailed out into the Brooklyn sky. Jenna raced to the window to watch her friends.

"We're flying!" cried Susan.

"Fly, vacuum cleaner," Libby sang out.

It was the most exciting thing that had ever happened to Libby, Susan, or Jenna.

As they flew off into the air, the cord to the vacuum cleaner followed them until it was completely stretched out.

Then, with a pop, the plug flew out of the wall. Susan and Libby crashed to the ground.

Jenna ran down the stairs and outside to check on her friends. "Are you all right?" she asked, leaning over Susan and Libby.

Susan groaned and sat up. "What happened?"

"I guess it doesn't work if it isn't plugged in," Jenna explained. Libby stood up and brushed the dirt from her dress.

"I'm never going to pass this test," she said sadly. Then she picked up the vacuum cleaner and walked into the house.

Susan looked at Jenna, her eyes twinkling. "It was great," she said. "Like being a bird. I can't believe witches get to do it all the time."

"Libby can't," Jenna reminded her. Susan looked at her friend.

"We have to come up with another idea, Jen. We just have to."

Fourteen

"I've got it!" cried Jenna, racing into the garden of Libby's house. Susan and Libby looked up from their lemonade.

"I was sitting in the dentist's chair—" said Jenna.

"Yuck!" Susan interrupted.

Jenna continued, "—and suddenly, it came to me. I know why you haven't been able to fly, Libby."

"Why?" asked Libby and Susan at the same time.

"It's the spell!" said Jenna.

The smile disappeared from Libby's face. "I don't think so," she said. "But thanks for thinking about it so much."

Jenna poured herself a glass of Libby's

special lemonade and sat down at the table.

"It has to be the spell, Libby," she said. "I'm sure of it."

"Why are you so sure?" Susan asked, chewing a piece of sugary lemon rind.

"Because of what Libby said about the cape," Jenna explained. Libby and Susan looked at each other. Sometimes Jenna was impossible to understand.

"Remember what you said, Libby?" Jenna asked. "That maybe the reason the cape didn't work was because you said the wrong spell?"

"I did say that," said Libby. "But it was just a guess."

"I think it was a great guess!" Jenna was getting really excited. She got up from the table and walked around the garden while she talked.

"None of the ways you've tried flying have worked, right?"

"Right," said Libby.

"And you've used the same spell every time, right?"

"Yeah," said Libby. "It's the spell I'm supposed to use."

"How do you know?" asked Jenna.

"It's the basic spell for flight in my book upstairs."

"Maybe it only works for certain things," said Jenna. "Maybe you need a different spell. I think you should check your spell book."

Jenna stood in the center of the garden, grinning like crazy. Libby didn't think she was right. But she didn't want to disappoint her new friend, so she went upstairs and got her spell book.

Susan and Jenna heard the yell a moment later. They raced into the house and up the stairs. Libby was sitting on the bed in her room, looking at a book called *Spells*. When Susan and Jenna entered the room, Libby looked up and grinned.

"Jenna, you're a genius!" she said.

"What does the book say?" Jenna asked.

"There's this really, really small print under the spell," said Libby. "I guess I didn't see it before."

"Well? What does it say?" asked Susan.

Libby read from the book. "Do not ride on objects that fly with this spell. The spell is not strong enough. Objects cannot carry weight."

"I knew it!" said Jenna.

"So this spell is only to make the objects fly," said Susan.

Libby nodded her head. "I need a different spell so I can fly *on the object.* I need a stronger spell!" Suddenly, Libby looked sad. "Where am I going to get a spell that strong?" she said.

Now it was Susan's turn to grin. "What about one of those books downstairs?"

"You mean Aunt Aurora's spell books?" said Libby. "I don't think so."

"Why not?" asked Susan. "Aren't you allowed to use them?"

"It's not that," said Libby. "The spells in those books are really strong. I've never used one before."

"You want to pass the test, don't you?" asked Susan.

"Yeah," said Libby. "But . . ."

"But what?" said Jenna. "I think it's a great idea!"

Libby took a deep breath. Then she looked at her friends. "Why not?" she said.

Moments later, the three friends were in the basement looking through Aunt Aurora's books.

"Look!" cried Susan, holding up a book. It was small and red, and it fit in the palm of Susan's hand. On the cover of the book was one word: *Flying.*

The girls went through the whole book, looking for the perfect way for Libby to fly. Susan really wanted to try a flying sled. But Libby said the spell was too hard. A flying car would be too hard to hide. The spell for a flying saucepan took three days. They were almost at the last page of the book when Libby shouted, "This is perfect!"

"I agree!" cried Jenna.

"Let's do it!" said Susan.

The friends stood up from the table. The time had come for Libby to fly. They were going to conjure flying shoes.

Less than an hour later, the three girls were in the basement making a brew to dip Libby's shoes into. They used the bottled ingredients from Aunt Aurora's shelf, caught a few flies, and dug up some bugs. It took them the whole afternoon. By dinnertime, they had the brew bubbling. Then it was time for Libby to chant the spell. She stumbled the first few times, because she was nervous. But with the help of her friends, Libby finally chanted the spell and waved her arms just the right way. The brew was now ready for the shoes.

Jenna read from the spell book:

"Dip them three times fast
and three times slow,
then turn around
as if to go."

Libby dipped and turned.

"Now turn once more
the whole way round,

hold the shoes
and touch the ground."

Libby followed the directions and waited for Jenna to read on.

"Dip one last time
and leave them in
until the sun has
set again."

"I don't understand," said Susan. "Is she supposed to leave them in until tomorrow?"

"Shhh," said Jenna. "Let her do this part first." Libby dipped the shoes in the brew, and the three girls met in a corner of the room to figure out what to do next. Jenna read the last part of the directions out loud.

"When the sun has sunk,
when the moon is full,
remove the shoes
and let them cool."

Susan giggled. "Sort of like chocolate-chip cookies," she said.

Jenna read on:

*"When the wings on the shoes
are clear and dry
put the shoes on
and whisper 'FLY.' "*

"That's it," said Jenna, closing the book. "I guess we leave the shoes in the brew until sunset."

"But sunset today or sunset tomorrow?" said Susan. "It isn't clear enough."

"And speaking of clear," said Libby. "What does 'clear and dry' mean? And what wings are they talking about?"

Jenna raised the shade on the basement window and looked out. "Well, the sun hasn't set yet," she said. "So I think we can take them out tonight after the moon has risen."

"Oh, no," said Susan. "What time is it?"

Jenna looked at her watch. "It's six-thirty. Why?"

"I have to get home for dinner," said Susan.

"I guess I should go home, too," said Jenna. "Libby, will you remember to take the shoes out when the moon is full?"

"Sure," said Libby. "But I still wish I knew what 'clear' means. And what about the wings? Were we supposed to put bird wings on the shoes?"

"I don't know," said Jenna. "We can only hope we did it right."

"When's your next test?" asked Susan.

"Friday night," said Libby.

"Today is Tuesday," said Jenna. "That should give you plenty of time to learn how to use your new shoes."

"*If* they work," said Libby.

"They just have to," said Susan. But even she wasn't so sure Jenna's idea would work. After all, Libby really wasn't very good at being a witch, and she probably said the spell wrong.

The three girls said good-night and promised to meet at Libby's house the next morning before school. As they closed the basement door, they could hear the brew bubbling and spitting in the darkened room.

Fifteen

Susan woke the next morning to a loud banging at her window. She jumped out of her bed and lifted the window shade. Then she jumped back in surprise. Libby was smiling at her right through the second-story window. She looked as if she was sitting on air. Susan opened the window and leaned out.

"Look!" said Libby, pointing at her feet. "Little wings. And they're totally colorless. That's what it meant. Clear wings!"

"LIBBY! YOU'RE FLYING!" shouted Susan.

"I know." Libby grinned. "Isn't it great? I've been practicing ever since the shoes cooled down at about four o'clock this morning."

"Didn't you sleep?" asked Susan, yawning.

"Who needs to sleep," said Libby happily. "I can fly!"

With that, Libby disappeared from sight. Susan leaned out the window a little farther and saw her friend flying among the trees. With a little kick of her right foot, Libby turned left and dived past Susan's window. A double kick with both feet made her rise far into the sky, and pointing her toes brought her back down to the ground. She banged into a few trees, and her landings were pretty awful, but Libby was flying. There was no doubt about that. With a little—no, a lot—of practice, Libby would be ready to pass the test Friday night.

The three girls met after school every day that week. With the help of Susan and Jenna, Libby learned how to control her shoes. By Friday, she could fly without banging into even one tree.

The test took place in Prospect Park. Susan and Jenna weren't allowed to go to the park at night, and they couldn't very well tell their parents what was going on. So they waited at Susan's house for news from Libby. When Libby didn't call by nine o'clock, Jenna went home.

The next day, Susan and Jenna went over to Libby's house. Aunt Harriet answered the door.

"Hello, dears," she said, smiling. "Why don't you go out to the garden?"

"Oh, no," Susan whispered to Jenna as they walked through the house. "The last time Libby was in the garden, she was crying."

"I know," said Jenna. "And she didn't call last night. I guess this means she has to go to that school." Jenna shivered at the thought of spending life as a lizard.

"I really thought the shoes were going to work," said Susan sadly. They walked out into the garden, but Libby wasn't there. A few minutes later, Aunt Harriet appeared with a pitcher of her now-famous lemonade.

"Libby will be down in a minute." She smiled. "I'm glad she's found friends like you two." Then Aunt Harriet disappeared. Susan and Jenna looked at each other.

When Libby walked into the garden, Susan almost dropped her lemonade.

"Libby, what happened?" Jenna couldn't believe her eyes. Libby sat down and smiled.

"I crashed into a tree and broke my hand," she said, holding up her right hand, which was in a cast. "That's why I didn't call last night. We had to go to the hospital." She started to laugh. "Aunt Aurora wouldn't go near the place, but Aunt Harriet put on this old flowered skirt she has and took me to the emergency room. It isn't that bad. The doctor said I only have to have the cast on for two weeks. Besides, I write with my left hand."

Susan was confused. "Why did you have to go the hospital?" she asked Libby. "Couldn't one of your aunts just zap your hand and make it better?"

Libby shook her head. "It doesn't work that way with broken bones," she said. "You need a special broken-bone powder, and Aunt Aurora didn't have any left." Libby smiled happily at her friends.

"Why are you smiling?" Jenna asked Libby. "I thought you didn't want to go to that witch school."

"I *don't* want to go," said Libby. "And I don't have to!"

"You mean—" began Jenna.

"I PASSED THE TEST," shouted Libby. "Even Aunt Aurora said one crash should be allowed at a test. And they couldn't believe how well I could fly."

Susan and Jenna jumped up to hug Libby.

"You haven't even heard the great news," Libby said, overcome with joy. "My aunts said because you two were so much help, you can help me with my other lessons if you want to."

"If we *want* to," said Susan. "Are you kidding?"

"What's the next test?" asked Jenna.

Libby got that funny little grin on her face again. "I have to turn myself into an animal," she said.

"A lion!" cried Susan.

"A zebra," yelled Jenna.

"A zebra?" Susan and Libby said at the same time. The three girls started to laugh.

"I have a great idea," said Susan. "How about if we start a club? We can meet every day after school and help Libby. It will be our own private club and no one else can join."

"Especially Annabelle Sloan," said Libby.

"Yeah!" said Susan.

"Great idea!" said Jenna. "Hey—what should we call ourselves?"

Libby thought for a minute. "How about the 'Three Little Witches'?" she finally said.

"I don't know," said Jenna. "Suz and I aren't really witches."

"But you'll be helping me," said Libby. "And you'll be in on all the witchcraft."

"I like it," said Susan. "Besides, no one will know what we're doing or what we call ourselves."

"Okay. Why not?" Jenna had to agree with her friends.

Libby picked up her glass of lemonade and raised it in the air. "To the Three Little Witches!" she said.

Susan and Jenna raised their glasses.

"The Three Little Witches," said Susan.

"The Three Little Witches," said Jenna.

They tapped their glasses together and chewed their lemonade.

What magic will the three little witches brew next? Find out in Book 2: *Three Little Witches and the Shrinking House*